D1517134

800 l

WORLD OF THE BIZARRE

Written by:
Stuart A. Kallen

Published by Abdo & Daughters, 6535 Cecilia Circle, Edina, Minnesota 55439.

Library bound edition distributed by Rockbottom Books, Pentagon Tower, P.O. Box 36036, Minneapolis, Minnesota 55435.

Library of Congress Number: 91-073059   ISBN: 1-56239-042-2

Cover Illustrations by: Tim Blough
Interiors by: Tim Blough

Edited by: Rosemary Wallner

TABLE OF CONTENTS

TRULY BIZARRE

The world is full of unexplainable mysteries. Even with modern science, computers, and experts on every subject, some phenomenon that simply cannot be explained. Indeed, many people deny that these mysteries even exist. Fire-walkers, rains of fishes, and human combustion are just some of the events that defy explanation. But it is a strange and mysterious world, and thousands of people have witnessed or taken part in puzzling episodes that are beyond the realm of human understanding. Every day, somewhere in the world, strange oddities continue to bewilder and amaze.

These strange events are called bizarre. The word "bizarre" is a little bizarre itself. The word is the same in almost every language, but it comes from the Basque language — spoken only by people in the Pyrenees Mountains between France and Spain. In that region of the world, very few men wear beards, and bizarra means "bearded one." Because of this rarity, "bizarre" came to mean "rare and fantastic." The Basque language is different from any other language in the world — another unexplained mystery.

For an event to be considered bizarre, it must be extreme, incredible, outrageous — BUT TRUE! However amazing or absurd they may seem, these events really have taken place.

As long as humans have existed, they have marveled at wondrous coincidences, rare occurrences, and bizarre calamities. With all the miracles of science, you might think that there would be very little left that is unknown. But happily, that is not true. For what would be the joy of life if we knew how *everything* worked? It's time to probe into these oddities ourselves, and try to explain the unexplainable, understand the unknowable, and explore the wonders of the bizarre.

¹bi•zarre\bə-'zär\ *adj* [F, fr. It *bizzarro*] (ca. 1648) : strikingly out of the ordinary: as a : odd, extravagant, or eccentric in style or mode <appears out of a ~ frog-shaped tent —Henry Hewes> b : involving sensational contrasts or incongruities *syn* see FANTASTIC — **bi•zarre•ly** *adv* — **bi•zarre•ness** *n*

BIZARRE NATURE - STRANGE RAINS

Every year, at the beginning of the rainy season, people in Yoro, Honduras, gather together buckets, barrels, and pails to catch the fish that will soon rain from the sky. Each year, for as long as anyone can remember, hundreds of thousands of sardines have fallen from the heavens when the rains begin. The shower of bright, silver fish usually begins in late afternoon and is followed by strong winds and electrical storms. The flying fish flop forlornly until they die. These stormy sardines are just one of the thousands of recorded incidents of amazing rain.

The first written mention of strange rains is probably in the Bible, where stones rained on an Amorite army and a plague of frogs rained on the Egyptians. The Bible also mentions manna, or food, raining from Heaven to feed the starving Israelites who were lost in the desert.

Ancient historians write of black dust, huge chunks of ice and burning objects falling from the sky. These events probably have natural causes like hail, volcanos, and meteors. But in 1578, yellow mice rained from the sky in Bergen, Norway. The next year, it rained fish in Bergen.

As if animals weren't strange enough, weird substances have been know to fall from above. In Naumburg, Germany, on March 23, 1665, a blue fibrous substance resembling blue silk rained down in great quantities. In 1696, a foul-smelling, butter-like substance rained down upon southern Ireland. The Bishop of Cloyne called it a "stinking dew" that was "soft and clammy, and of a dark yellow color." People in Kilkenny, Ireland, thought it was useful medicine and saved it in buckets and pails.

Rains of wool-like substances, silk, and thread have also been recorded. Strange jello-like goo has rained down in Ireland, Germany, and other countries. In Philadelphia, Pennsylvania, on the night of September 26, 1950, two police officers saw something fall from the sky. When they stopped to examine it, they saw a domed disk of quivering purple jelly, six feet in diameter and one foot thick. It glowed in the dark. When the men tried to pick it up, it dissolved in their hands, leaving a sticky, odorless scum. Within thirty minutes, the whole thing had evaporated.

No reasonable explanation has ever been given for this space jello.

The list of strange rains is endless. In 1796, on the island of Haiti, a huge quantity of black eggs fell from the sky. They hatched the next day, and some of the sky-animals were preserved in water. They shed their skin several times and resembled tadpoles. In 1794, a deluge of toads fell in Lalain, France. The toads were the size of walnuts and began to hop in every direction when they landed. Toads have rained all over the earth and continue to do so on rare occasions today. Fish, lizards, spiders, turtles, and snakes are all common creatures that have fallen like rain from the sky. Scientists guess that these creatures are caught up in strong winds and remain in clouds for weeks before they fall to the ground, but no one seems to know for sure.

Perhaps the strangest creatures to rain down to earth were the five humans who fell out of a thundercloud and onto a mountain in Germany. The men, frozen in ice, were glider pilots who had been carried into a cloud by strong air currents. When they bailed out of their planes, they became the nucleus for giant, human hailstones.

The list of strange rains is endless. Toads have fallen
from the sky all over the earth.

People with sweet tooths were happy when candy rained from the sky in Lake County, California, in 1857. The shower of sugar happened on two different nights and local women made syrup from the powder. Another California oddity took place on August 1, 1869, when flesh and blood fell for three minutes on a two-acre farm in Los Nietos. The day was clear and windless, and the flesh fell in fine particles, and in strips from one to six inches long. Fine hairs also fell. Apparently, no one bothered to make *that* into dinner.

More meat rained down over a 5,000-square-yard area in Bath County, Kentucky, on March 3, 1876. The sky at the time was cloudless when four-inch squares of fresh meat began to fall. Two men bravely tasted it and thought it was venison or mutton. The meat was analyzed and it turned out to be lung material from a horse. No explanation was given for its origin. In the more appetizing category, green peaches the size of golf balls fell from the sky in Shreveport, Louisiana, on July 12, 1961. It was not recorded whether anyone bothered to bake them into a pie.

We've all heard of pennies from heaven, and sometimes money does fall from the sky. People in central Russia were pleased when silver coins rained down in August 1940. In Bristol, England, in 1956, hundreds of pennies rained down on a group of school children. Thousands of 1,000-franc notes fell in Bourges, France, in 1957. No one claimed the notes or reported a theft. Bank-notes valued at 2,000 marks (about $1,500) fluttered down from a clear sky in Limburg, West Germany, in 1976. The money was picked up by two clergymen. A carpenter in Dusseldorf, Germany, was not so lucky in 1951. He was working on a roof when a shaft of ice six feet long fell from the sky and impaled him. He died instantly.

Money has been known to rain down from the sky.

BIZARRE HUMANS -
FIRE-WALKERS

Night has fallen on the island of Fiji. A harvest
ceremony is being held beneath the swaying
palm trees. Natives dance, sing, and play drums
in the wild, tropical night. A pit six feet deep
and twenty-five feet long had been dug in the
ground. Stones and logs had been piled into
the pit in the days before the ceremony. The
logs were set aflame and had been burning for
over twenty-four hours. As the dancing becomes
faster and wilder, the logs burn to ashes, and the
temperature of the red-hot stones is now about
eight hundred degrees. No one can get near the
pit because of the intense heat.

The men in the tribe assemble before the pit, and
a final prayer is offered. The leader of the group
walks directly to the fire pit and casually strolls
around the pit on the searing stones. The rest of
the group follows. The natives are barefoot and
have a slightly difficult time keeping their balance
on the stones. Their faces show no flicker of
emotion. After several unhurried minutes of
walking on the red-hot stones, the fire-walkers
leave the pit. As they do, the onlookers break

into wild applause. The ceremony is over until next year, and the men have suffered no harm.

In 1950, a doctor examined the feet of Fijian fire-walkers before a ceremony. He found that the natives' feet were sensitive to a burning cigarette and a pinprick, and were not covered with any protective substance. The doctor examined the feet after the fire-walk and found that they were covered with ashes, and just as sensitive. When asked about this amazing phenomenon, the leader of the walkers said, "the water god sent hundreds of water babies to spread their bodies over the stones, and the men walked on the backs of the cool water babies."

Such is the power of belief. The fire-walkers had known since they were children that someday they would walk on fire. They believed in the water babies and never thought about being burned. One man who tried the fire-walk in 1940 but was not prepared mentally was burned so bad that both his legs had to be amputated.

People walk on fire in many parts of the world, including Hawaii, India, Japan, and Haiti. Native Americans of the Navajo tribe dance on fire in New Mexico, and Christians in the Greek town of Langadas walk on fire during the feast of St. Constantine. In some parts of the world, fire-walkers go through intense rituals and prayers, and walk on coals in a trance. In some places, people just scamper across the fire without any preparation.

Sometimes, bystanders will join in on a whim, such as E.G. Stephenson, an English Professor who was watching a Shinto fire-walking ceremony in Tokyo, Japan. Stephenson wanted to try fire-walking for himself, but a priest insisted he prepare himself first. The priest took him to a temple and sprinkled salt over his head. Then Stephenson took the walk. The professor said he felt only tingling on his feet as he walked across the red-hot rocks. At one point he did feel a slight pain, and when he examined his feet later, he realized that he had cut his foot on a sharp rock. This was the only pain he received from the event!

Perhaps the strangest fire-walking event took place in Madras, India, in 1920. The ceremony was conducted for a maharaja (a Hindu prince), who had a man bless the walkers before they entered the fire pit. Some people went voluntarily, while others had to be pushed.

*A priest blessed the firewalkers before
they entered the pit.*

A man who was watching the ceremony described how the people who were pushed had looks of terror on their faces that gave away to astonished smiles as they realized that they would not be burned. Finally, the maharaja's band was told to march through the coals. They did so, and enjoyed themselves to such a degree that they decided to march through again, this time playing their instruments. With cymbals clashing, trumpets blowing and drums pounding, the band marched across the scorching coals. According to witnesses, flames rose up, licking their instruments and faces, yet their boots, uniforms, and even sheet music were all untouched by the fire.

The reasons for fire immunity are unknown, but the history of fire-walking is filled with many gruesome deaths and injuries. This is obviously not something that one would try at home! But as long as the human mind continues to search for power over nature, fire-walkers will continue to cross the heated fires into the zone of the unknown.

BIZARRE HUMANS -
FIRE IMMUNITY

While some people walk through fire pits on special occasions, some people are resistant to fire every day of their lives. These exceptional people have a natural resistance, or immunity, to fire, and they can do things that would cause normal humans to burn horribly.

The most famous example of fire immunity is the case of Nathan Coker, a former slave and a blacksmith who lived in Easton, Maryland, in the late 1800s. While many fire handlers need to go into a trance to handle fire, Coker needed no preparation to handle scorching heat. According to the *New York Herald* dated September 7, 1871, Coker was tested before several city officials. First, a shovel was heated to white-hot in a coal oven. Coker then pressed the scorching shovel to his bare feet for over fifteen minutes. An examination of his feet by a doctor showed that no harm had been done. Coker then reheated the shovel and laid the red-hot iron on his tongue! Coker also *drank* red-hot, molten lead and swished it around in his mouth, over his teeth and gums, until it became solid. He picked burning coals out of the fire and held a red-hot poker in his hands. Coker told the amazed officials, "I don't burn. Since I was a little boy, I've never been afraid to handle fire. "

History is full of people with fire immunity who became entertainers to amaze and astound audiences. One well-known European entertainer from the late 1600s was known as Richardson. In his act, Richardson chewed burning coals and swallowed them, drank melted glass and wax, and held burning iron in his mouth. Apparently though, women found his kisses less than appealing.

People who can cause fires with just the power of their touch are called "fire genies." One celebrated case of a human torch was that of A. W. Underwood of Paw Paw, Michigan. Underwood could take a handkerchief and rub it and breath on it, and cause it to burst into flames. He could also start paper on fire with his breath. He said it was useful on camping trips, where he could start a campfire in minutes. No mention is made of *his* kissing abilities.

History is full of people with fire eating abilities.

BIZARRE HUMANS - BURSTING INTO FLAMES

The opposite of fire immunity is called "spontaneous combustion" — people bursting into flames for no reason. When they found Mrs. Thomas Cochrane, all that was left of her was seated in an armchair in which she had fallen asleep. Cochrane had been burned beyond recognition, but neither the pillows nor the cushions of her chair were scorched. In October 1959, 19-year-old Maybelle Andrews was dancing with her boyfriend in a London pub. Suddenly, she burst into flames. The fire blazed on her back and her chest, igniting her hair. Her boyfriend tried to put out the flames but could not. Maybelle died on the way to the hospital. Investigations stated that there were no candles burning and no one was smoking near Andrews. Her boyfriend testified that the flames originated *within* her body.

These are just two of the hundreds of cases where people have suddenly burst into flames for no reason. Usually these people are reduced to ashes within minutes while their clothes and the surrounding area are untouched by the fire. Spontaneous human combustion (SHC), is such a bizarre phenomenon because the human body is extremely resistant to burning. If people are cremated after they die, they are put into flames of over three thousand degrees for four hours. Sometimes, even then, the burning is not complete. Over two hundred people have been recorded as victims of spontaneous combustion over the past four centuries, but science has never had an answer or explanation for the causes of this human oddity.

One of the earliest recorded cases of SHC is of a poor woman in Paris in 1763. The woman was a heavy drinker and had not eaten solid food in three years. One night she went to sleep, and in the middle of the night, she burst into flames. All that was left in the morning was her head and fingers. The rest of her body had been reduced to ashes.

A rather strange case of spontaneous combustion was recorded in England in 1788. A man entered a room in his home and, to his amazement, he saw his young chambermaid scrubbing the floor with a fire blazing on her back. The man cried out in alarm. It was only then that the chambermaid realized what was happening and began to scream. She was dead before the fire could be

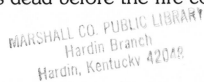

put out. No candles or flames were burning in the room at the time.

Many victims of SHC are people between seventy and ninety years old. One woman who burst into flames was 114 years old. The youngest known victim of SHC was eleven-month-old Peter Seaton of London, England. The youngster was put to bed as usual in January 1939, when a visitor, Harold Huxstep, heard screaming from the boy's room. Huxstep rushed to the bedroom to find Peter engulfed in flames. The intense heat threw Huxstep against the wall. There was no chance of rescuing the boy. Firemen arrived, but by then Peter was badly burned. There was no known cause of the fire and, despite the charring heat, nothing else in the room was damaged.

Spontaneous combustion was such a well-known phenomenon in the eighteenth and nineteenth centuries that it was mentioned in books by a number of famous authors. In Charles Dickens' *Bleak House*, Krook, a mean old man, dies gruesomely of spontaneous combustion. In Herman Melville's Redburn, Miguel, a stranded sailor, is found on board a ship, burning as the horrified crew looks on. Melville writes, "two threads of greenish fire, like a forked tongue, darted out between the lips, and in a moment, the cadaverous face was covered by swarm of wormlike flames...the uncovered body burned before us, like a phosphorescent shark in a midnight sea."

A number of causes for spontaneous combustion have been suggested but none have been proved. Among them are fireballs from space, lightning, internal atomic explosions, microwaves, and high-frequency sound. How any of these events might work are unexplained. And, for now, so is spontaneous human combustion.

spontaneous combustion *n* (1809) : self-ignition of combustible material through chemical action (as oxidation) of its constituents — called also *spontaneous ignition*.

BIZARRE HUMANS - ELECTRIC PEOPLE

People in the modern world are used to the power of electricity. We know that it is generated at power plants and sent through wires to our homes. But there are some people who are human electrical generators, and those who have this mysterious power can have some high-voltage problems.

The first known electrical person investigated by scientists was fourteen-year-old Angelique Cottin, of La Perriere, France. Cottin's strange condition began on January 15, 1846, and lasted ten weeks. The slightest touch from her hand or her dress would cause heavy furniture to spin away or jump up and down. Any objects that Cottin approached retreated from her. Compasses spun wildly in her presence. A study group was appointed by the respected French Academy of Sciences. The scientists decided that Cottin's power came from electromagnetic electricity. The power was stronger in the evening and seemed to emanate from her left side. Cottin was terrified by the whole thing, and was very happy when the power left her.

*Angelique Cottin had a strange condition; the
slightest touch from her hand would cause heavy
furniture to spin away or jump up and down.*

Another electrically charged case from France was a baby who was born in Saint-Urbain in 1869. The infant badly shocked all who touched him, and luminous rays shot from his fingers. When he died at the age of nine months, a glow was observed around his body.

In the 1890s, teenager Jennie Morgan of Sedalia, Mississippi, was highly charged. Sparks flew from her to nearby objects, and people forgetful enough to shake her hand were often knocked unconscious!

Caroline Clare, seventeen, of London, Ontario, became very ill in 1877. Her weight dropped dramatically, and she suffered fits during which she described far-off lands that she had never seen. When she recovered about a year later, she was electrified. Metal objects that came in contact with her became magnetic, and stuck to her skin. This became rather disturbing at dinner time, when forks, knives, and spoons had to be pried off of her. Her strange condition was reported by the Ontario Medical Association in 1879.

Another electromagnetic person was Frank McKinstry of Joplin, Missouri. When McKinstry was feeling charged, he had to keep moving, because if he stopped, his feet would become glued to one spot. When this happened McKinstry had to ask passers-by to lift his feet and release the charge. Although dozens of cases of electric people have been written about and studied by scientists, no explanation has ever been given for this bizarre phenomenon.

Some people have been known to become magnetic; metal objects stick to their body.

One man's strange condition only affected him when he was in church. He would suddenly fly into the air.

BIZARRE HUMANS - OTHER ODDITIES

Time and space does not allow a complete list of all the strange and weird mysteries known to be unknown. There are people who glow in the dark like fireflies. Some people can fly, and one man, Joseph de Copertino, would suddenly fly into the air during church services. He was banned from public worship and was very embarrassed whenever he took off towards the ceiling.

Most people can't fly, but some possess an extraorinary sense of balance. In the early 1880s, an acrobat known as Blondin walked on a tight-rope stretched over Niagra Falls. The sure threat of instant death did not bother Blondin, and he repeated his exploit while pushing a wheel-barrow containing another man. Blondin stopped in the middle, and with the falls crashing below, cooked and ate a meal one hundred feet above the crashing waters! Blondin died peacefully in bed after his last high-wire performance. He was seventy-three-years-old.

Certain people attract lightning. Major Summerford was struck by lightning on a battlefield in Flanders in 1918. This event left him paralyzed from the waist down. He moved to Vancouver, Canada, and was hit by lightning in 1924. This event paralyzed his right side. Summerford was struck again in 1930, and he died two years later. In 1934, during a thunderstorm in Vancouver, lightning hit a tombstone in the cemetery, shattering it to pieces. The tombstone was Major Summerford's! The man attracted lightning even in death.

There are thousands of other cases of horribly bad luck. The wedding day of Princess Maria della Cisterna in Turin, Italy, on May 30, 1867, was marred by these events: Her wardrobe mistress hanged herself; the palace gatekeeper cut his throat; the colonel leading the wedding procession collapsed from sunstroke; the stationmaster was crushed under the wheels of the honeymoon train; the king's aid was killed when he fell off of his horse; the best man shot himself. The couple did not live happily ever after.

Certain people attract lightning. Major Summerford was struck by lightning 3 times, and his tombstone was even hit by lightning.

ALL'S WEIRD
THAT ENDS WEIRD

So what does it all prove? Well, it's hard to say. One book can't begin to explain all the outrageous oddities of history. After all, the finest scientific minds have been furiously debating these strange events for hundreds of years. All we can do is enjoy the feeling of pure wonder at these startling events. And we can all be glad that we aren't about to burts into flames. Hopefully.

Maybe one day soon, you'll look out your window and see fish, frogs, and fruit raining from the sky. When that happens, get your strongest umbrella from the closet, and remember, all's weird that ends weird!